MW01043458

Mahmoud Meets Moses

by
John J. Zwald
and
Diane O. DesRochers

Illustrations by John Zwald

Mahmoud Meets Moses
©2012 by John J. Zwald and Diane O. DesRochers

First printing

This is a work of fiction. Names, characters, places and incidents either are the product of the author's imagination or are used fictitiously. Any resemblance to actual persons, living or dead, events or locales is entirely coincidental.

ISBN - 978-0-9838832-9-6

Published by
WRB Publishing
Palm City, FL 34990
wrb1174@att.net

Printed in the United States of America

To my daughter Reneé Zwald

It was a beautiful warm day when Mahmoud and his father arrived at the airport in Cairo, certainly a far cry from the cold winter in Syracuse, New York where they lived. Mahmoud's father, Irahin, always wanted his son to visit family in Egypt, but funds were not sufficient for them to travel until now.

A total of 5634 miles.

The family often drove to New York City to see the Statue of Liberty and skyscrapers like the Empire State Building

His family enjoys looking at the City of New York and would like Mahmoud to compare the cities he will see in Egypt

The family drove to Kennedy Airport for their flight to Egypt.

They boarded the plane around six in the evening but wouldn't arrive in Cairo for nearly eleven hours. Most passengers slept during the flight, except for Mahmoud's dad who was so excited to see his brothers and to show off his only son.

Irahin's brother, Saide, agreed to meet them upon their arrival in Cairo. Since the family spoke little English, Mahmoud's father insisted his son speak some Egyptian Arabic, so he could greet his relatives properly.

"As salam alykum," said Mahmoud.

"Wa alykum e salam. Ahlan wa sahlan," responded Uncle Saide. (Hello and welcome).

Mahmoud shook hands with his uncle. "Zein al Hamdulillah?" (I'm fine thanks, and you?).

The uncle chuckled. "Zein al Hamdulillah?" (I'm fine too, thanks).

Nine-year-old Mahmoud was amazed at how things looked in Cairo. Big evergreen trees were replaced by palm trees and sand dunes took the place of grass. The boy was happy to run around his uncle's farm. He talked to all the animals there, but was especially fond of a small burro that seemed to smile whenever Mahmoud spoke to him. Mahmoud named him Moses.

"Moses," said Mahmoud petting the burro, "this place is very different from where I live. It's really hot here. And to think I wanted to bring my winter jacket with me."

"Hee haw," brayed the burro.

"So you think that is funny? I do too." Mahmoud laughed along with Moses.

Moses did many jobs around the farm. Mahmoud thought the small burro was mistreated when he pulled the cart to the city with the whole family riding in the back, even though Uncle Saide told his nephew Moses was strong and could carry most anything.

Mahmoud was happy when Uncle Ali, his father's older brother, came to the farm to see the American boy. Ali rode a large camel, covered with beautiful rugs of bright colors. It strutted with an air of royalty. Alongside this camel was a smaller camel, carrying gifts. Mahmoud liked that camel right away although he noticed that Moses backed away from the visitors, almost like he didn't want to be compared to the great camels.

When Uncle Ali gave the smaller camel to Saide, Mahmoud was happy. "Now Moses won't have to do all the work," exclaimed Mahmoud. "It's only fair that camels do the necessary farm work too," he told his uncle who reluctantly agreed.

One day a government truck came to the farm to pick up Moses, along with many other burros from the area as they were needed to carry heavy equipment for work on the canal.

The family was upset to give up Moses. "We'll return him," promised the government official, but Mahmoud was afraid they'd mix him up with someone else's burro.

"Can we please tie a red ribbon around Moses' neck?" asked Mahmoud. "That way they'll know which burro belongs to us."

Mahmoud was unhappy now that Moses was gone. He missed him so much.

Uncle Saide and his wife Ahneri were to go on a short business trip. "Would you like to come with us, Mahmoud?"

Of course the young boy was happy to go to the city. After sightseeing and shopping, the three enjoyed a meal of Mazza, Ahysh, Khubz, and Gamar (appetizers, fish, bread and a delicious drink) before heading home.

That evening as they watched the news on television there was an announcement. "There has been a horrible accident on the Suez Canal," said the reporter. "One worker was killed and three others are now trapped in the water, under a crane. It seems that a barge crashed into the crane, causing it to topple into the canal."

"How awful," said Mahmound. "I hope they can save them from drowning."

The following day news came that a small burro had saved the lives of the three men. "One small burro, standing near a coil of rope saw the danger to the workers and kicked the end of the rope out from under the wreckage. With his strong teeth, Moses grabbed hold of the rope and with the assistance of a workman standing nearby helped pull them back to safety." It showed a picture at the scene.

"Hey Dad, that's Moses," yelled Mahmoud. "Look, he's still wearing his red ribbon."

Sure enough, it was Moses. The government proclaimed the burro to be a hero.

"Hooray Moses, you are home again," said Mahmoud. "Do you know that you are a hero?"

Moses shyly smiled.

Soon it was time for Mahmoud and his father to return to the United States. The family, along with the Egyptian hero, Moses, was allowed to go out on the tarmac to the airplane to say goodbye.

Mahmoud hugged his relatives goodbye, then turned to Moses and gave him a big kiss. Moses smiled.

The family left the scene very happy and all were proud of their super hero, Moses.

"Ma'a salama!" called Mahmoud, as he waved goodbye.

Moses smiled again, then brayed,"Hee haw, hee haw."